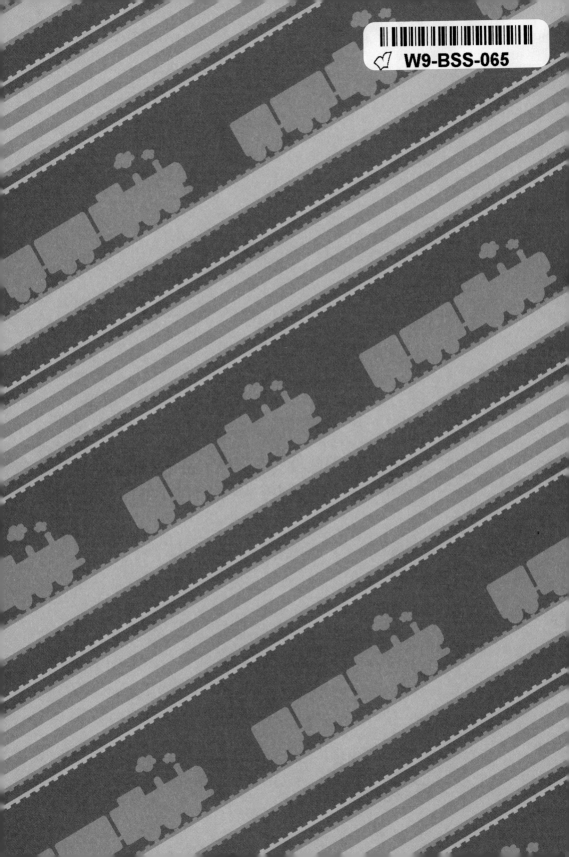

Thomas the Tank Engine & Friends

A BRITT ALLCROFT COMPANY PRODUCTION
Based on The Railway Series by the Rev W Awdry
Copyright © Gullane (Thomas) LLC 2001

www.randomhouse.com/kids   www.thomasthetankengine.com

Library of Congress Cataloging-in-Publication Data:
A crack in the track : a Thomas the Tank Engine story / illustrated by Tommy Stubbs.
    p. cm.
"Based on the Railway series by the Rev. W. Awdry."
SUMMARY: A crack in the track brings Thomas the Tank Engine and the entire Island
of Sodor Railway to a screeching halt in this rhyming adventure.
ISBN 0-375-81246-6 (trade) — ISBN 0-375-91246-0 (lib. bdg.)
[1. Railroads—Trains—Fiction. 2. Stories in rhyme.]
I. Stubbs, Tommy, ill. II. Awdry, W. Railway series.
PZ8.3 .C8398 2001 [E]—dc21 00-053330

First Edition

Printed in the United States of America   December 2001   20

A CRACK IN THE TRACK

A Thomas the Tank Engine Story

Based on *The Railway Series* by the Rev. W. Awdry

Illustrated by Tommy Stubbs

BEGINNER BOOKS
A Division of Random House, Inc.
New York

Thomas was a little blue steam engine.
He lived on the Island of Sodor
with many other engines.

Sometimes Thomas pulled his coaches,
Annie and Clarabel.

"Hurry, hurry!" said the coaches.

Sometimes Thomas pulled freight cars.

"Faster, faster!" said the foolish freight cars.

They would try to push Thomas down the hill.

And sometimes Thomas traveled
all by himself across the island.

He chugged in the rain.

He huffed in the sun.

And he puffed in the snow.

"There is nothing a train cannot do!"
Thomas said proudly.

One morning, Henry the Green Engine
would not come out of his shed.
He had boiler ache.

So Sir Topham Hatt asked Thomas to help.
"Peep, peep," Thomas said to the people.
"I can take you where you want to go!"

Soon clouds gathered.

The sky grew dark.

Thunder rumbled.

Plip. Plop. CLUNK.

Hail began to fall!

It fell on Thomas.

It fell on the tracks.

Suddenly, Thomas' driver
saw trouble ahead.
"Slow down!" said the driver.

The hail had made a crack
right there in the track!
Thomas came to a stop.
His driver called out,
"We cannot go forward,
and we must not go back."

"Everyone off!" the conductor said.

"Now what shall we do?"
said the people.

They climbed down from the coaches
and climbed up to the road.
Bertie the Bus was just passing by.

Bertie beeped his horn merrily.

"A bus is as good as a train!" he said.

"I can take you where you want to go!"

All the people climbed on board Bertie.

Bertie scooted down the road.

"A bus *is* as good as a train,"

the people said.

Suddenly, Bertie's driver
saw trouble ahead.
"Slow down!" the driver said.

There in the road
was a bright green toad.
Bertie came to a stop.
His driver called out,
"There's a toad in the road!
We will have to unload."

"Everyone off!" said Bertie's driver.

(That toad in the road

caused a fuss on the bus.)

"What will happen to us?"
the people said.

Then they walked down the road
to another train station.

But the trains were not running.
"Why not?" asked the people.
They soon found out.

Thomas was still stuck
at the crack in the track.
Percy was stuck there at Thomas' back.

Gordon was stuck
behind Thomas and Percy.

James, with two freight cars,
was in quite a hurry.

The freight cars were needed in the yard.
But James could not get past
Gordon and Percy and Thomas.

And the foolish freight cars refused
to back up.
"No, no, no!" they said.
"We will not go!" they said.

So no trains could move up.

And no trains could move back.

They were stuck where they were
at that crack in the track!

"I guess there are some things
that a train cannot do," said Thomas' driver.
"We need help," said Thomas.
"And I know just who to call."

Thomas' driver called Sir Topham Hatt
and told him Thomas' plan.
"An excellent plan!" Sir Topham said.
"Please thank Thomas," he added.

In no time at all,
Harold the Helicopter
zoomed across the sky.

He landed near the people.

They all climbed aboard.

"A helicopter is

as good as a train!" said Harold.

"I can take you

where you want to go!"

The breakdown crew came
to replace the broken track.
By the time they arrived,
rain was falling hard.

The crew came with cranes.

They sang while they worked.

"A crane is as good

as a bus or a train.

We'll fix up your track,

and we don't mind the rain."

Finally, Thomas could move.
So could Percy and Gordon.
James, with his freight cars,
was close behind.

They turned on the turntable
and went back to work.

The people saw Thomas
waiting to take them home.
"Are you *sure* you can take us
where we want to go?" they asked.

"I thought there was nothing
a train could not do," said Thomas.
"But now I know that just isn't true.
I learned a big lesson from one little crack.
A train is only as good as its track."

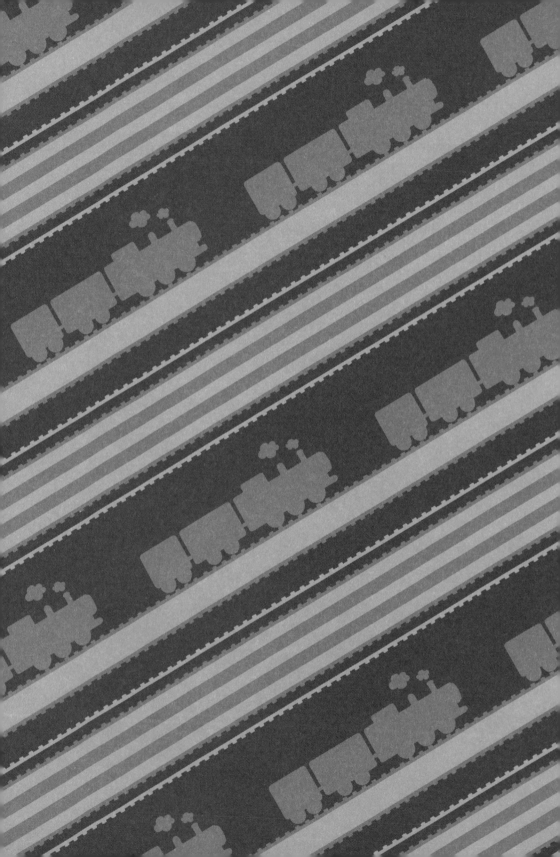